The Great Big
Enormous Turnip

THE GREAT BIG ENORMOUS TURNIP

COLLINS
PICTURE LIONS

PICTURES BY HELEN OXENBURY
STORY BY ALEXEI TOLSTOY

First published in Great Britain 1968 by William Heinemann Ltd
Published in Picture Lions 1988

Picture Lions is an imprint of the Children's Division,
part of the Harper Collins Publishing Group,
8 Grafton Street, London W1X 3LA

Illustrations © Helen Oxenbury 1968

Printed by Warners (Midlands) plc, Bourne and London

Once upon a time an old man planted
a little turnip and said,
"Grow, grow, little turnip, grow sweet. Grow,
grow, little turnip, grow strong."

And the turnip grew up sweet and strong,
and big and enormous.
Then, one day, the old man went to
pull it up.
He pulled and pulled again, but he could
not pull it up.

He called the old woman.

The old woman pulled the old man.
The old man pulled the turnip.
And they pulled and pulled again, but they
could not pull it up.

So the old woman called her granddaughter.

The granddaughter pulled the old woman,
The old woman pulled the old man,
The old man pulled the turnip.
And they pulled and pulled again, but they
could not pull it up.

The granddaughter called
the black dog.

The black dog pulled the granddaughter,
The granddaughter pulled the old woman,
The old woman pulled the old man,
The old man pulled the turnip.
And they pulled and pulled again, but they
could not pull it up.

The black dog called the cat.

The cat pulled the dog.
The dog pulled the granddaughter,
The granddaughter pulled the old woman,
The old woman pulled the old man,
The old man pulled the turnip.
And they pulled and pulled again, but still they
could not pull it up.

The cat called the mouse.

The mouse pulled the cat,
The cat pulled the dog,
The dog pulled the granddaughter,
The granddaughter pulled the old woman,
The old woman pulled the old man,
The old man pulled the turnip.

They pulled and pulled again, and up
came the turnip at last.